By Arie Kaplan

Illustrated by Meg Dunn

A GOLDEN BOOK • NEW YORK

Published in the United States by Golden Books, an imprint of Random House Children's Books, a division of Penguin Random House LLC, 1745 Broadway, New York, NY 10019, and in Canada by Penguin Random House Canada Limited, Toronto. Golden Books, A Golden Book, A Little Golden Book, the G colophon, and the distinctive gold spine are registered trademarks of Penguin Random House LLC.

rhcbooks.com

Educators and librarians, for a variety of teaching tools, visit us at RHTeachersLibrarians.com

ISBN 978-0-593-57045-6 (trade) — ISBN 978-0-593-57046-3 (ebook)

Printed in the United States of America

10 9 8 7 6 5 4 3 2 1

Marty McFly was a cool teenager. He lived in a pleasant town called Hill Valley in the year 1985. His parents were George and Lorraine McFly.

Marty went everywhere on his skateboard.
But he would soon find a *new* way to travel.

Marty's best friend was an inventor named Doc Brown. One day, Doc showed Marty his latest invention. It was a **time machine**—made from a car!

The car looked very futuristic. Doc explained, "If you're going to build a time machine into a car, why not do it with some style?"

Marty was very excited. He jumped into the time machine—and accidentally turned on the time circuits.

"Great Scott!" Doc shouted.

Before Marty knew it . . .

. . . he had traveled back in time! Marty was now thirty years in the past! He was in *1955.*

"This has got to be a dream," he said. The time machine had landed inside a barn. The farmer who owned it was *not* happy.

Oh, no! The time machine was broken. Marty was stuck in 1955! He knew that Doc Brown was a young scientist back then, so he went to the doctor's lab.

"Doc, you're my only hope," Marty said. Young Doc thought about how to help Marty get back home.

In the meantime, Marty had to find a way to fit in with the other kids in the past.

Soon Marty met a teenage boy. "I'm George," the boy said. "George McFly." Marty broke out in a cold sweat. He couldn't believe it. George was his dad!

Marty also met a girl named Lorraine. She was Marty's mom! Marty didn't tell them that he was their son from the future. They wouldn't believe him!

Biff was the town bully.

"What are *you* looking at?" he shouted at Marty. The big bully chased Marty, but Marty got away!

Marty's antics caught Lorraine's eye, and she forgot all about George! Marty had to do something. He needed her to fall in love with George—otherwise Marty wouldn't exist in the future!

Marty had an idea. He told George to ask Lorraine to the school dance.

"I'm George McFly," George told Lorraine. "I'm your density. . . . I mean, your *destiny*."

George and Lorraine danced. They really liked each other. Marty was happy. His parents would get married!

Marty decided to play some rock music from his time on a guitar. But it was too loud for the 1955 teenagers!

"Guess you guys aren't ready for that yet," Marty said with a shrug. "But your kids are gonna love it."

Marty had other things on his mind anyway. He had to figure out how to get back to his own time!

Doc Brown explained that only a bolt of lightning could generate enough electricity to power the time machine. Fortunately, Marty knew from Hill Valley history that lightning would strike the town's clock tower that very night!

So Doc made a plan! He attached a cable to the clock tower, then he attached a metal hook to the time machine.

Doc told Marty, "We're going to send you back to the future!"

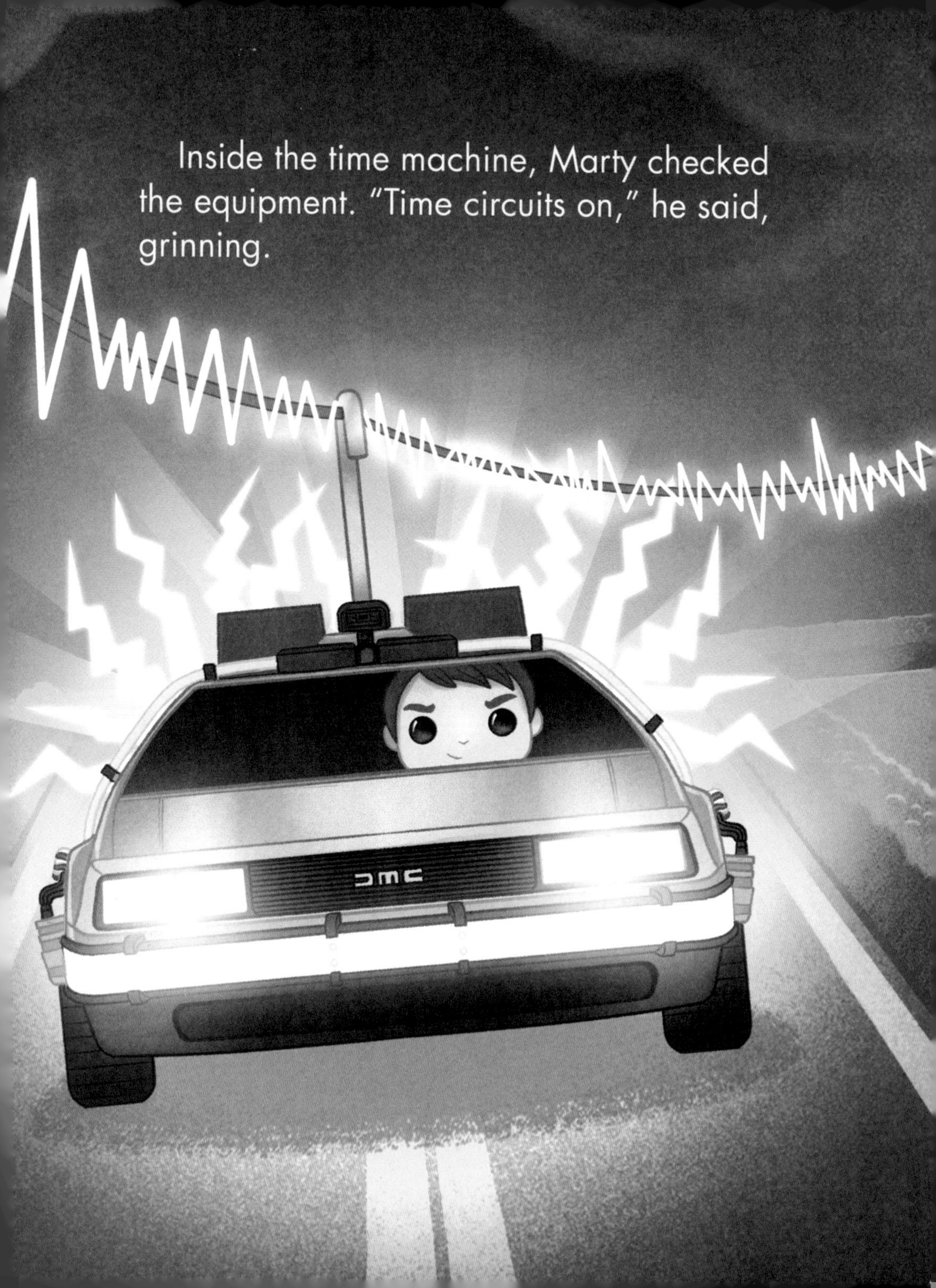

Inside the time machine, Marty checked the equipment. "Time circuits on," he said, grinning.

ZAP! Lightning hit the clock tower. The lightning crackled as it darted toward the cable.

The time machine zoomed toward the cable. When the hook and cable touched—*ZZZZZAP!*—the time machine disappeared in a flash of light!

SUCCESS! Marty reappeared in his own time! And older Doc Brown was right where he'd left him.

“It works!” the doctor exclaimed.
The two friends cheered.

Marty thought his time-traveling adventures were over . . . until Doc Brown later appeared in an upgraded time machine from the future. Marty's adventures were just beginning!